U0054783

華 文 俳 句 集

渺 光 之 律

洪郁芬 著

Tune of Tiny Light
Chinese Haiku Anthology

Yuhfen Hong

序一

相同於日本「俳句大學」的國際學部，以提倡「切」與「兩項對照組合」的二行華文俳句個人詩集「渺光之律」的台灣出版是值得慶賀的。

俳句原是日本的傳統詩型之一，現已跨越日文藩籬，在世界各地以不同的語言書寫，儼然成為國際性的文學型式。然而，綜觀國際俳句的實況即可理解，大部分的國際俳句都寫成三行，卻無表現俳句美學的實質內容。這是因為國際俳句對於俳句的形式與特色沒有達成共識所致。

為了於華文圈提倡俳句的本質「切」與「兩項對照組合」，並推廣俳句，我擔當顧問及作者參與洪郁芬、郭至卿、趙紹球、吳衛峰於二○一八年十二月《華文俳句選》的出版。除此之外，也擔當成立於二○一八年十二月四日的「華文俳句社」的顧問，力圖華文俳句的推廣與發展。

003

身為「華文俳句社」的顧問，我相當樂見華文俳句社社長洪郁芬出版《渺光之律》俳句集。希望此俳句集的出版能使讀者更理解「切」與「兩項對照組合」的俳句美學，並冀望華文俳句能與古典詩、現代詩、小詩、散文詩等齊聚一堂共同豐富華文詩壇。

踢飛蚱蜢前進

草千里

這是洪郁芬入選日本第二屆「二百十日」俳句大會的俳句。能與專業的日本俳人一同領獎，不只證明她的日文素養高深，也說明了她俳句藝術之不凡凡響。

近年來洪郁芬刊登日本「火神」俳句雜誌，並於「火神」六十五號（平成三十一年春號）被火神主宰今村潤子評選「渺光之律／草露」。今村氏如此評道：「將草露粟米般的光以『渺』來形容，並看見渺光中包含的音律。因而可知作者獨特的觀察力與細膩的情感。」

鳥囀

喚來行舟渡輪

扭開玻璃瓶鋁蓋

臨夏

秋日麗

門示意即開

以上這幾首俳句，無論是在內容，或是在季語的兩項對照組合使用上，完全不亞於日本正規俳句。我敢斷言，洪郁芬完全符合能在日本俳句界發展的條件。

愛之盡

白蟻的黑羽滑落

歲初閱覽新約聖經

愛的文字

我們從這幾首俳句感受郁芬鮮明的青春魅力，無疑是她俳句的一大特質。除了愛之「盡」外，「蒲公英棉絮／夢裡草原的盡頭」等，句集裡出現多次的「盡頭」，如：

山路盡頭之極

櫻花開

回望山路盡頭蔚藍的海

歲之行始

對於「盡頭」的喜好和追求，也可以說相通於對「那方」或「彼方」，甚至是對於「結束後的世界」有濃厚的興致和傾向。

魚鱗雲

地球彷彿那方

來世今生的糾葛

冬靄

從這兩首俳句，我們彷彿進入洪郁芬的心靈花園，藉由俳句來鋪陳。字裡行間的宗教信仰或是對來世的觀感，也可說是她俳句的一個特點。

最後列舉幾首我心所慕的俳句：

庭戶如我

落花無數

鞦韆的高點捕獲

童年

蝴蝶飛

盡全力的輕巧

孩童爭吵打破碗

大暑

日本俳句協會副會長、日本俳句大學校長、俳人

令和元年七月吉日

永田満德

永田満德先生簡歷

俳人、日本俳句協會副會長、俳人協會熊本縣分部長、日本俳句大學校長、雜誌《未來圖》同人、雜誌《火神》總編輯。由恩師引領開始創作俳句三十年至今。在文學研究方面，著有對三島由紀夫和夏目漱石俳句的論考。著有《寒祭》（文學の森）、《漱石熊本百句》（合著，創風出版）、《新くまもと歳時記》（合著，熊本日日新聞社）。

序一

日本の「俳句大学」の国際俳句学部が提唱している「切れ」と「取り合わせ」を取り入れた二行俳句の華文圏初めての個人句集『渺光之律』が台湾で出版されることは大変喜ばしいことである。

俳句は日本の伝統的な詩の一つである。今では世界各地でそれぞれの言葉で書かれている国際的な文学形式である。しかし、三行書きにしただけの俳句は形式のみで、俳句の美学を表現しているとは思えない。それは俳句の型と俳句の特色に対する共通認識がないからである。

そこで、日本俳句の大切な美学である「切れ」と「取り合わせ」の二行書きの俳句を提唱し、華文圏での俳句の発展に寄与するため、私は顧問および作者として洪郁芬、郭至卿、趙紹球、呉衛峰と共に二〇一八年十二月に台北で《華文俳句

010

選》を出版した。さらに二〇一八年十二月四日に創立した「華文俳句社」の顧問になり、華文俳句のさらなる進展を図ってきた。

「華文俳句社」の社長である洪郁芬氏が句集『渺光之律』を出版することは「華文俳句社」の顧問として楽しみである。なぜならば、この句集によって、「切れ」と「取り合わせ」の俳句の美学に対する理解が深まり、絶句（漢詩）、現代詩、短詩、散文詩などの様々なジャンルを持つ華文詩の中で、華文俳句の定着と広まりがより一層華文詩界を豊かにすることが期待されるからである。

　　　　きちきちを飛ばして進む草千里

掲句は第二回「二百十日」俳句大会に入賞した句である。日本の専門俳人の中で入賞したことは洪氏の日本語能力の高さを示すばかりではなく、俳句においても並々ならぬ力量を持っていることを證明した。

最近では、日本の俳句雑誌「火神」に参加し、積極的に投句している。「火神」六十五号（平成三十一年春号）で、今村潤子主宰は「ちっぽけな光の調べ草

の露」を選び、『草の露』の栗粒のような光を『ちっぽけ』といい、更にそれが調べをなしているというところに作者の感性の細やかさがある。」と評している。

噂りや呼ばれて出づる渡し船

硝子瓶蓋をひねれば夏近し

秋うらら合図のやうに開くドア

これらの句は内容の雰囲気といい、季語との取り合わせといい、日本の俳句にさおさ劣らない。洪氏は日本の俳壇でも十分通用できると言っても過言ではない。

恋の果て白蟻の羽黒く落つ

初読の新約聖書愛の文字

洪俳句のみずみずしい青春性が感じられる句で、作者の俳句世界の一面を形作

っている。

ところで、「恋の果て」と同様に「たんぽぽの絮草原の果の夢」とあるように、「果て」の文字を使った句がいくつも出てくる。

山道の果ての果てにも桜咲く

初旅や山路の果ての青き海

「果て」の句には「果て」なるものへの嗜好が読み取れる。この「果て」への嗜好が「向こう」、あるいは「あの世」への志向へと繋がっていると言ってよい。

うろこ雲向こうに地球あるやうな

もつれ合ふあの世とこの世冬の靄

この二句からも窺われるのは、洪氏の独特な精神世界、つまり俳句世界が描き出されていることである。この宗教的とでも言える彼岸意識は洪俳句により深み

を与えていて、洪俳句の特色をなすものである。

最後に共鳴句を挙げておきたい。

あの庭と同じ落花のしきりなり
ブランコの高みで捕らふ幼き日
全力の軽やかさなり胡蝶飛ぶ
皿を割る子供の喧嘩大暑かな

令和元年七月吉日

日本俳句協会副会長、日本俳句大学学長、俳人

永田満徳

永田満徳氏プロフィール

俳人、日本俳句協会副会長、俳人協会熊本県支部長、俳人協会幹事、日本俳句大学学長、「未来図」同人、「火神」編集長。恩師の紹介で俳句を始めて三十

午、現在に至る。文学研究では三島由紀夫や夏目漱石の俳句などの論考がある。句集に『寒祭』（文學の森）共著に『漱石熊本百句』（創風出版）『新くまもと歳時記』（熊本日日新聞社）。

序二

渺光之律，源於我的一首在日本火神句集被評論的俳句，「渺光之律／草露」。先不談此俳句字面上的意思，來談剛起步的華文俳句。於古體詩、現代詩占絕大多數的華文詩圈中，是的，過去的俳句只是米粒般渺小的存在，是台灣文學日治時代以來的遺產，是上流社會長輩們的社交消遣，是現代詩人創作小詩的一個選擇。俳句在華語文學的汪洋大海中是極顯微的，是小眾中的小眾。然而究竟甚麼原因，讓殖民時代遺留下來的外來文體，能不停的被傳揚而不隱沒？

以殖民的影響來概述俳句的影響力，似乎違背國際俳句發展之趨勢。自十九世紀後半以來，歐美的日本研究者將俳句擴展至全球舞台，已經達到令人難以想像的規模。數百年來，俳句不僅未隨時代的變遷消失，至今仍普及於各國文藝界，詩人們相繼探尋以本國語言創作俳句之可能性。近來因為諾貝爾獎詩人，瑞典的托

馬斯・特蘭斯特羅默（Tomas Transtömer）也寫俳句詩，更助長了國際文壇的俳句風。因此，俳句的影響力非但不小，更有甚者，儼然已成為國際文壇的通用文體。

回頭來談渺光之律。草露之渺小，如同華文俳句形式之短小。在「世界最短詩型」的俳句中，華文俳句更是短小，幾乎是海灘的沙粒了！詹冰提倡減字定型俳句，以三四三共十字。而華俳的規則是寫成兩行，無字數限定，因此可長可短。且看此句集的夏之首，「愛或不愛／花已葉」，共七字，或是此俳句詩集的書名緣由，秋之首渺光之律，共六字。當然，好的華文俳句非以字數的多寡評論，如同其他詩體一樣，是心弦的震動，是字間彷彿若有光。

光的旋律。一個秋天早晨，我行走於霧裡的市民農場。反照的路鏡蒙蓋整個清晨的灰。環繞家園的遠山忽隱忽顯。在沉默的灰白和漫無邊境的影子裡，我看見路旁的小草各個結了粟米般的露珠，閃耀著光的旋律。其音清脆飽滿，像自行發光的小恆星高聲頌揚全能者奇妙的造化。此時我想起俳句。在忙碌繁雜的日常生活中，我們的眼光常受到思緒的影響，看不見季節的變化，只關注於纏繞自己的是非。有時候我們過度專注於數點發生的種種失去，而看不見當下所擁有的美景。然而當我們願意停下腳步靜觀生活中的萬象，試圖從所有的不堪中尋找美好之處，或觀照季

節裡發生的事物並書寫成俳句，這些瞬間的感動便如草露的光律，在生命中發出清脆的聲響，成為我們存在的確據。

亨利・柏格森（Henri-Louis Bergson）說過，生命取決於記憶或直覺的時間。當我們隱藏於剎那的經驗中，此曇花一現的片刻便有了恆常的意義。我們擺脫了時間的限制而自由，在每個瞬間燃燒一生。俳句即是捕捉瞬間靈思，化為永恆的一種文學形式。俳人靜觀生活中的萬象，試圖從中看出美好。此即日本美學的「物哀」（もののあはれ）。飛花落葉，松濤麥浪，稍縱即逝的生命中，唯有瞬間的觀照成為存在的證據。以一年為週期的「季語」讓我們切實意識到時間的流動。一個「切」（切れ）促使我們停下來觀察傾聽景物的脈動。而我們所寫下的俳句，會在同樣關注語言藝術的人群中，引起一種特別的共鳴曲調，如草露之光律相互震盪。

日本俳人正岡子規曾經主張「寫生」概念。他說日本文學史中，上世階段表現主體美感的文學較多，後世則愈加深入表現客觀美的境界。「不直敘成為結果的情感，惟注重描寫作為原因的客觀事物，從而打動讀者。」當我們專注於凝視外界，內在的真與外界的真協調了，混合了，我們消失，而達到一個更大的光明——與萬化冥合。我們在自然裡，自然也在我們裡。於是，樹即是你，你即是樹。此般形神

雨忘的境界，便是渺小如草露般的俳句所釋放的，與永恆與萬物冥合的光之旋律。

期盼此俳句詩集的誕生，能使讀者更了解華文俳句，並且能在日常生活停下腳步，將剎那的感動化為永恆。最後，容我以英國詩人威廉·布萊克（William Blake）的「純真的預言」（Auguries of Innocence）之開頭作為此序文的結語：

一顆沙裡看出一個世界，
一朵野花裡一個天堂，
把無限放在你的手掌上，
永恆在一刻那裡收藏。

二〇一九年五月吉日

洪郁芬

序二

　書名「渺光之律」は、私が火神句集で評論された俳句「ちっぽけな光の調べ草の露」に由来します。まずこの俳句に触れずに、創立したばかりの華文俳句について語ります。古体詩、現代詩が多数を占める華文圏で、初歩の階段にある華文俳句は米の粒ごとにちっぽけな存在です。俳句は台湾の殖民地時代の遺産であり、上流社会の年配の方の娯楽であり、現代詩人の数多い創作法の中の一つです。華語の文壇が広い海であるとすれば、俳句はその中で泳ぐ一匹のイルカのような小さい存在です。しかし、何故俳句はちっぽけながらも台湾で書き続けられてきたのでしょうか？

　殖民の影響で俳句を略述するのは、俳句の国際発展現状と相違するでしょう。十九世紀以来、欧米の日本研究者のおかげで、俳句の世界的影響は小さいどころか著しいものです。ここ数百年間、世界各国の詩人たちが自分の国の言語で俳句

の創作を意欲的に試みています。近年はノーベル賞を受賞されたスウェーデンのトーマス・トランストロンメル（Thomas Tranströmer）が俳句詩を書くため、世界の文壇で俳句は大いに注目されています。俳句は世界的影響が大きいばかりではなく、もはや国際に共通する文体であると断言しても宜しいでしょう。

俳句は世界で一番短い詩である。華文俳句はさらに、その中でもっとも短い俳句と言えます。詹冰の減字定型俳句は十文字に限定している。華文俳句の規定は一行書きのみで、字数の制限がないため、短いものは漢字六文字しかありません。例えば、「渺光之律／草露」。しかし、華文俳句は短いながらも、一瞬の感動を永久に変える文芸です。草の露の光のように、早朝の薄明かりの中でもちっぽけながら輝いています。

アンリールイ・ベルクソン（Henri-Louis Bergson）は、物理的な時間ではなく、記憶に裏打ちされ質的に多様な体験的時間である「持続」（durée）こそ生の実相だと言いました。時間の制限を抜け出し、それぞれの瞬間に燃える生き方は俳句と同じように、一瞬を永久に変える存在の證です。俳句は瞬間を永久として生きる人たちの中で共鳴を成し、小さな露の調べのように心を震わせるでしょう。

021

写生を中心とし、物を読む文芸である俳句によって、作者と読者は万物を凝視し、そしていつか自我も消えて万物融合するという真の光に溶け込む。ちっぽけな草露の光が姿かたちも精神もを忘却し、日光に溶けて消えてゆくように。

最後に、この句集により、華文圏の多くの方が華文俳句を理解し、日常の中で立ち留まって、瞬間の感動を永久にする俳句を書くようになれば幸いです。イギリスの詩人、ウィリアム・ブレイクの『無垢の予兆』の冒頭でこの序文を締め括ります。

　　一粒の砂には世界があり
　　野に咲く花には天国があり
　　きみの手は無限をつかみ
　　永遠のひとときを得る

二〇一九年五月吉日

　　　洪郁芬

CONTENTS

春

Spring

庭戸如我
落花無數
あの庭と同じ落花のしきりなり

garden there and I

continuous fall of petals

蔫然佇立靈山
白木蓮

霊山にふと立ち止まる白木蓮

suddenly stopped at the holy mountain
white magnolia

初櫻

光一滴滴散落

初桜光のしづく散らしたる

first cherry blossom of the year

light scattered drip by drip

蒲公英棉絮
夢裡草原的盡頭

たんぽぽの絮草原の果の夢

a floc of dandelion

end of grassland in the dream

崇山峻嶺的懷裡仰望

春耕

仰ぎたる山の懐春耕す

look up to the high mountains and lofty hills

spring ploughing

春日後晌
媽祖揮動拂塵
春の昼媽祖の拂塵を振つてゐる

spring afternoon
Mazu's whisking her whisk

盡全力的輕巧
蝴蝶飛

全力の軽やかさなり胡蝶飛ぶ

to be light at full strength

butterflies fly

福壽草

融冰的片刻

福寿草冰を溶かすひとときに

amur adonis

the moment ice melted

八掌溪

數著鳥巢渡過

鳥の巣を数へて渡る八掌溪

crossing and counting birds' nests

Pachang River

一龍昇天

愛河的主燈

龍天に登る愛河の主燈かな

a dragon climbing into the sky

main lantern of the Love River

以平靜的時刻為家

一日春

安らげる時は我が家や春一日

take peaceful moments as home

a spring day

夜櫻
從不追究離別

夕桜別れの気配見咎めず

cherry tree in the evening
do not follow up the parting

卡特來蘭馥郁
外科診所

カトレアの馨る外科医の診察室

sweet-smelling cattleyas

a surgeon's clinic

少年的機車引擎

閻魔賽日

少年のバイクエンジン初閻魔

motorcycle's engine of the youth

Yama's temple fair

擦拭仰角的玻璃

喇叭花裙

仰角の硝子窓ふく花フレア

clean the glass window overhead

flower flare skirt

將寂寥細綁成束
風信子

侘しさを一束にしてヒアシンス

tie loneliness into a bundle
hyacinth

狂歡節
渴望戴上面具的臉
謝肉祭仮面かけたき真の顔

Carnival

a face wants to put on a mask

無色的謐靜中停息

花夜

色のなき靜けさにゐる花の夜

rest in the colorless quietness

night of flowers

靴韆的高點捕獲

童年

ブランコの高みで捕らふ幼き日

catch my childhood

swing at the highest point

清明

歌頌賢母的壽域墓

清明や賢母を語る合祀墓

Pure Brightness

assembly tomb recounting wise mothers

木窻柳青

紀州庵

紀州庵木窓に柳青むなり

Kishu An Forest of Literature

willows green by the wood windows

山中池

蝌蚪的白眼直視

山の池蝌蚪の目白くにらみたる

lake on the mountain

tadpoles glowered with white eyes

蓬萊毛茛

不問山為人知否

人知れぬ山であらうと金鳳花

despite the mountain is unknown

buttercups

山路盡頭之極
櫻花開

山道の果ての果てにも桜咲く

at the end of the mountain road end

cherry blossom bloomed

闇眼即是深山林木

明媚春日

目閉じれば深山の森うららけし

a deep forest when I close my eyes

lovely sun

鐵路黯淡的鈴聲
櫻花雨

鉄道の呼び鈴鈍し花の雨

dull bell of the railroad

rainning petals

學生眼眸灼灼星光
復活節

教え子の目に光る星復活祭

stars shine in students' eyes
Easter Day

鳥囀

喚來行舟渡輪

囀りや呼ばれて出づる渡し船

chirps of birds

set off the awakened ferry

初戀慢慢地遠

春虹

初恋の遠のいてゆく春の虹

my first love became distant

spring rainbow

披著清晰的日影

風信子

鮮やかに日陰をかぶる風信子

She's brightly covered with shade

hyacinth

春驟雨
擋風玻璃繪圖

春驟雨フロントガラスに絵を描く

drawing pictures in the front glass

spring shower

巨木比文字恆久
燦爛的風

文字よりも永久の巨木や風光る

giant tree older than words

breeze shines

春分

一半的人生

春分や真ん中くらいの餘生なり

the Spring Equinox

half way of life

一城的樹騷動
春疾風

騒ぎ立つ一城の木々春疾風

All trees make a noise in the town

spring gale

飛落可安歇的水邊

風箏

飛び降りる憩いの汀いかのぼり

jump down to the quiet waters

kite

雨後山峰薄雲半掩

婦女節

隱したる薄雲の峰女性の日

peaks covered with clouds

Women's Day

惜春

孔雀嘶啼摺羽

惜春や鳴いて孔雀の羽収む

regretting the passing of spring

a peacock ululates and folds wings

扭開玻璃瓶鋁蓋

臨夏

硝子瓶蓋をひねれば夏近し

When I twist the lid of glass bottles

near summer

夏

Summer

愛或不愛
花已葉
愛しても愛さなくても花は葉に

love or not

flowers turned into green leaves

阿拉卡列的爪趾一躍

夏日至

アラカリのかぎ爪跳ねて夏来る

jumping claw toes of aracari

summer comes

繞著一生的歲月浮游
海月水母

一生の時を浮遊す水海月

go round and round a lifetime

jellyfish

攜手下坡

麥秋

繋ぎ手で下る山道麦の秋

go down the hill hand in hand

wheat harvest

愛之盡
白蟻的黑羽滑落

恋の果て白蟻の羽黒く落つ

end of love

fallen black wings of termites

直等到那日

螢火灼灼

いつしかと来たらむ蛍火きらきらす

eagerly waiting

twinkle light of a firefly

洗髮

那些成泡沫流逝的

泡泡に流れ去るもの髮洗ふ

hair washing

things that flowed past like bubbles

戴戒指的手緊握

蛇莓

蛇苺握りしめたる指輪の手

mock strawberry

a ring hand grasped tightly

泳装
光的網襪透明

海水著透ける光の網タイツ

bathing suit

fishnet tights of sunlight

靈魂點燃即滅

姫螢

魂の光りて消ゆる姫螢

soul lit up and faded away

a firefly

紫陽花搖
遁入幽間細徑

紫陽花の揺れ細道に忍びたり

shaking hydrangea

hide in the narrow road

習得天籟之途
蟬聲

天籟の見習いありき蝉の声

halfway to learn the celestial sound

voice of cicadas

涼しさやピアノホールのエレベーター

鋼琴廳電梯下樓

清涼

cool and refreshing

the elevator goes down to the piano hall

同我旋轉的螺

潮水夢

螺旋するさざえと同じ潮の夢

spiraling trumpet shell and I

tide in the dream

回眸的微笑
檸檬花

微笑みをかへす眼差し花檸檬

smile back with a gaze
lemon flowers

驟雨之島

最後的訪談不遇

島驟雨会へずじまひの見舞ひかな

torrential rain in the island

failed to meet each other in the last visit

一會即一生
初夏東風
一会とは一生のことあいの風

one encounter, one life

summer east wind

地下室冷氣

重金屬音樂

地下室のクーラーの音へビーメタル

air conditioner in the basement

heavy metal music

銀河

生命各自蛻變

銀漢や命ことごと蛻変す

milky way

life transforms respectively

星沫満天飛

水平線

満天へ星しぶき飛ぶ水平線

sea horizon

splashes star spry all over the sky

濃淡不一的光
游泳

濃淡の違へる光水泳す

different shade of light

swimming

孩子爭吵打破碗

大暑

皿を割る子供の喧嘩大暑かな

children fought and broke dishes

heat wave

華麗的背對背朝外
蝴蝶蘭

華やかに背に背を向けて胡蝶蘭

back to back gorgeously

moth orchid

夏日河川
跨越岩石無反顧

がむしゃらに石を飛び越し夏の川

crossover the stones reclessly
summer river

沉落煙囪的光束
暮夏

煙突に沈む光束夏の暮

beams sink in chimneys

summer sundown

蛇緩慢褪皮
余亦然

ゆっくりと蛇衣をぬぐ我もまた

Snakes peeled of their coats slowly

so do I

錦鯉的波浪搖晃
戀茶樓

色鯉の波に揺られて恋茶楼

jolted by the waves of varicolored carps

the Love tea house

秋

Autumn

渺光之律
草露

ちっぽけな光の調べ草の露

tune of tiny light

grass dew

夜夜堆疊的思慕
楓初紅

一夜ずつ重なる思ひ薄紅葉

yearnings overlapped night by night

light autumn leaves

秋うらら合図のやうに開くドア

門示意即開

秋光明媚

autumn sunny day

open the door with a sign

晨讀宋詞三百

白露

朝よりの宋詞三百白露かな

300 Song Poems in the morning

White Dews

秋雨滴答
獨奏蕭邦

秋雨のぽつぽつひとりショパン弾く

tick-tocking autumn rain

play a Chopin alone

一段情束手無策

仰月

ままならぬ恋の一片仰ぐ月

look up at the moon

a piece of love beyond control

邂逅與離別同日
秋彼岸

同じ日の出逢いと別れ秋彼岸

meet and leave in a day
the Autumnal Equinox

天堂鳥花低頭
居侍月

もたげたる極楽鳥花居侍月

bird-of-paradise flower dropped her head
moon went up slowly

極目遠望的故鄉

陣雨

見霽かす故鄉の日景時雨来る

hometown stretches to the horizon

drizzling rain

命是一世虚空
飄紅葉
定めてふ虚ろの一世紅葉散る

a vain life called destiny
autumn foliage scattered

遅疑不決的相會

暮秋

再会を見合はせる日や暮の秋

decline to meet again

late autumn

以人字飛往人地

侯鳥

人の地に人の字でゆく渡り鳥

to human's land in the shape of Chinese character human

migratory birds

魚鱗雲
地球彷彿那方

うろこ雲向こうに地球あるやうな

mackerel clouds

the earth is beyond

踢飛蚱蜢前進

草千里

きちきちを飛ばして進む草千里

Let grasshoppers fly and march on

a thousand miles grassland

巡湧泉參拜

阿蘇之秋

湧き水を巡り拝むや阿蘇の秋

tour the spring water and make a pilgrimage

autumn in Aso

可指望的事物之一

秋風

当てになる物のひとつに秋の風

One of the things I can count on

autumn wind

山野串聯著擦身的相遇
薏苡珠滿枝

すれ違ふ山野の出逢ひすずこ玉

passed by one on one encounters

beads of a rosary

紅毛港

丹娜絲叩門不進

紅毛港通り過ぎゆく野分かな

Hongmao Port

Dannas knocked and went away

冬

Winter

小寒

初讀聖經哀歌

寒の入聖書の哀歌読み初むる

slight cold

first time reading Lamentations in the Bible

山脊筆直

滑雪者波動

まっすぐな尾根や波打つスキーヤー

a straight ridge
undulating skier

衣著厚重的推銷員
待日出

著ぶくれのセールス日の出の待ち時間

thickly dressed salesman
waiting for the sunup

シーサーのマント時間を翻す

翻轉時間

風獅爺斗篷

a Guardian Lion's mantle

overturning of time

回望山路盡頭蔚藍的海

歲之行始

初旅や山路の果ての青き海

blue sea at the end of the mountain road

first trip of the year

歳初閲覧新約聖經

愛的文字

初読の新約聖書愛の文字

first reading of the New Testament

words of love

如兩項對照組合的咖啡

歲始俳會

取り合はせのやうなコーヒー初句会

blend coffee like Toriawase

first haiku gathering

烤蛤蠣萎縮
馨香滿溢

焼牡蠣の萎えてみなぎる香りかな

roasted shell clam shrank
flooding fragrance

湧流不息的泉源
歲之愛始
ほとばしる源ありき姫始め

There was a spurting source
first making love

初雪

溶成一滴涙

初雪や溶けて涙のひとしづく

first snow

melted into a teardrop

小春日
澄清湖翡翠蕩漾

小春日や翡翠流るる澄清湖

mild early winter

emerald ripples in the Cheng Ching Lake

不吝惜的鮮血沿著十架流下

聖誕紅

十字架で流す血潮やポインセチア

poinsettia

unstinted blood flowed along the cross

偷拍所有情節

浮水鴛鴦

鴛鴦や一部始終を隱し撮り

Mandarin ducks

secret photographing of the whole story

惋惜Ｓ尺寸牛仔褲
年前準備

惜しむべきＳのジーンズ年用意

regret the jeans of size S

preparation for the new year

來世今生的糾葛

冬靄

もつれ合ふあの世とこの世冬の靄

entangling afterlife and this life

winter mist

囲まれて群るる野ネズミ冬深し

暮冬

圍困的野鼠群集

surrounded wild rats began to flock

late winter

永久的祈禱不息

第一道曙光

永久になる祈りは絶えず初明り

never-ending eternal prayer

first dawn

附錄一　日本著名俳人五島高資評洪郁芬俳句三首

龍天に登る愛河の主燈かな

愛河は高雄市を流れる大河。その流れは龍の姿と重なる。李白の「黄鶴楼送孟浩然之広陵」における一節「惟見長江天際流」を思い出す。龍の瞳のような流燈の光が水平線の彼方なる天へ向かう。時まさに李白の詩と同じ仲春。龍は単なる河の流れではなく、躍動し始める万物の象徴である。龍と共に天に登る主燈は作者の心眼でもある。天人合一こそこの句の真骨頂である。

一龍昇天
愛河的主燈

131

愛河是貫穿高雄的大河。潺潺流水與龍的姿態相疊重合。我想起李白的「黃鶴樓送孟浩然之廣陵」之一節，「惟見長江天際流」的詩句。如龍的眼眸，燈流的光朝向水平線之外，那遠方的天際。時令恰巧是仲春，與李白的詩不謀而合。而龍不僅是流淌的河水，也是這個季節開始躍動的萬物之表徵。與龍一同升天的主燈可以說是作者的心眼。此俳句之最是體現天人合一的境界。

天籟の見習ひありき蝉の声

蝉の発する音を「声」として聴くことが出来るのは詩人の心耳である。虫の音の深奥にある天然の妙と同化することでもある。天籟、地籟、人籟の三要素によ る深い詩境に感銘する。

習得天籟之途
蟬聲

詩人心裡有個耳朵，將蟬的鳴音解讀為聲音。與之同化的是蟲鳴深處蘊含的，

那大自然的至善之妙。此俳句的詩境深邃，具有天籟、地籟、人籟的三要素，我深

受感動。

ちつぽけな光の調べ草の露

造化の妙は小さな草の露にも宿る。様々な露の光に音律を感じ取った作者の鋭

い感性に魅了される。視覚と聴覚による共感覚は、芭蕉の句にも見られ、しば

しば俳諧精神の至境を現出する。また、原句にある「律」の調べは、秋の趣から

「侘び」「さび」に通底し、一期一会の儚さがゆえに貴い感銘がもたらされる。

もっとも、日本人でもこうした俳諧精神の奥義に通達している俳人は多くない。

作者の俳句における造詣の深さに唯々驚くと同時に、さらなる詩境の展開が大い

に期待される所以である。

渺光之律

草露

造化之妙也寓于渺小的草露。我為作者能在露珠的光裡聽見音律，其豐富的感受性深深著迷。芭蕉的俳句裡也常見視覺與聽覺的互換，屢屢呈現俳諧精神的最高境界。另外，此俳句的「律」，也與秋天的情趣「寂寥」和「幽雅」共通，因一期一會的幻滅而帶來珍貴的感動。當然，日本人也很少能領悟俳諧精神的奧義。我為作者於俳句的深造備感驚訝，也因此相當期待她未來詩境的進展。

五島高資氏プロフィール

日本俳句協会副会長、日本文芸家協会会員、現代俳句協会会員、日本現代詩歌文学館振興会会員、日本内科学会会員、岩手県立千厩病院血液内科長、日本血液学会会員、国際俳句交流協会会員、宇都宮国際文化協会会員、国立博物館特別支援者、城見ヶ丘大学講師、俳句大学副学長、宇都宮大学非常勤講師。「全国学生俳句大会推薦大賞兼文部大臣奨励賞」、「第十三回現代俳句新人賞」、「第十九

回「現代俳句評論賞」、第一句集『海馬』にて中新田俳句大賞スウェーデン賞を受賞。句集に『海馬』（東京四季）、『雷光』（角川書局）、『五島高資句集』（文学の森）、『蓬萊紀行』（富士見書房）。「俳句スクエア」代表。

五島高資先生簡歷

日本俳句協會副會長，日本文藝家協會會員，現代俳句協會會員，日本現代詩歌文學館振興會會員，日本內科學會會員，岩手縣立千廄醫院血液內科長、日本血液學會會員、國際俳句交流協會會員、宇都宮國際文化協會會員、國立博物館特別支援者、城見ヶ丘大學講師、俳句大學副校長、宇都宮大學特約講師。曾獲「全國學生俳句大會推薦大賞兼文部大臣獎勵賞」、「第十三回現代俳句新人獎」、「第十九回現代俳句評論賞受賞」、第一句集《海馬》獲「瑞典獎」。著有句集《海馬》（東京四季）、《雷光》（角川書局）、《五島高資句集》（文學之森）、《蓬萊紀行》（富士見書房）。網路「俳句スクエア」代表。

135

附錄二　詩人秀實評洪郁芬俳句　算數秋風

詩人洪郁芬八月二十日於「華文俳句社」發表俳句作品如後：

算數秋風

可指望的事物之一

秋風

華俳作為華語詩歌的文類之一，其特點是：兩行式，前後的關係為切，季語。其情況猶如「商籟體」。既有形式我想指出是，華文俳句可歸類為格律體的新詩。其情況猶如「商籟體」。既有形式上的規限，也有內容上的要求。商籟體又名英式十四行詩，其最後兩行常為總結全

136

詩的精髓，是鞭辟的警句格言。華文俳句的其中一行是「干涉部」，另一行是「基底部」。後者為俳句的基本內容，而前者為對基本內容所提供的背景或指向。

洪郁芬這首俳句僅十個字。卻符合詩歌藝術上最高的法則——詩歌語言的建構。時下也有人主張五七五式的漢俳，但多措辭陳套，因襲古風，了無新意。這首俳句的基本內容為秋風。秋風乃氣體的流動，無形而可感。但詩人卻提供一個極其驚人的指向，「事物之一」，即詩人當下所接觸的眾多事物中的其中一項。而秋風非事物也不能以數量計。故其潛在語言是，所有的事物當下均無關宏旨，惟秋風撩人。何其悲愴無奈之意！

秋風撩人者何！詩人在非常局限的文字中提供了線索，「指望」。這個兩字詞用的極為巧妙，完全是一個具有悟力的詩人的用語。詩人獨立秋風中，感到存在的茫然。今夜燈火，明日關山，將歸何處！無指望的人生是悲痛的。而詩人所指望的卻杳有明言。我想起二〇一六年諾貝爾文學獎得主鮑勃迪倫(Bob Dylan)的歌辭：

The answer is blowing in the wind
答案在茫茫的風中

不明言是詩歌極其重要的技法之一。其理論是世間的事物不能盡言，所有的詩歌均為局部的呈現。秋風既為可指望的事物之一，其理即詩人仍相信有可指望事物的存在，為之二，為之三，只是當下她未曾發現。詩在悲愴中又隱存希望。此俳字字珠璣，推陳而翻新，意蘊糾結反復，餘味無窮！讀俳句，以「心」非以「目」，此之謂也。

二〇一九年八月二十二日

世界華文作家交流協會詩學顧問

秀實

秀實先生簡歷

世界華文作家交流協會詩學顧問，香港詩歌協會會長，《圓桌詩刊》主編。曾獲「香港中文文學獎詩歌獎」、「新北市文學獎新詩獎」、「昌耀詩歌獎入圍獎」等多個獎項。著有詩集《紙屑》（港版）《昭陽殿記》（港版）《臺北翅膀》

138

（台版），《像貓一樣孤寂（中英雙語詩集）》（港版），散文集《九個城塔》《蝴蝶不做夢》（大陸版），評論集《劉半農詩歌研究》（港版）《散文詩的蛹與蝶》（港版）《小鎮一夜蟲喧》（港版），小說集《某個休士頓女子》（港版）《蝴蝶不做夢》（大陸版），評論集《劉半農詩歌研究》（港版）《散文詩的蛹與蝶》（港版）《我捉住飛翔的尾巴》（大陸版）《為詩一辯》（台版）等。並編有《燈火隔河守望——深港詩選》（港版）《無邊夜色——寧港詩選》（港版）《大海在其南——潮港詩選》（港版）《風過松濤與麥浪——台港愛情詩精粹》（台版）等詩歌選本。

付録二　詩人秀実による洪郁芬俳句の評論

詩人洪郁芬は八月二十日於「華文俳句社」でこの俳句を発表した：

秋風を数へて

当てになる物のひとつに秋の風

華文俳句は華文詩の分類一つであり、その特色は二行に書き、そして前後の関係は切れと季語である。華文俳句は格律体の現代詩に帰することができ、ソネットと同じ状況であると思う。つまり、形式の制限もあり、内容の規定もある。

140

ソネットの別名は十四行詩で、最後の二行が全詩の精髄になり、大抵激励する格言で終わる。華文俳句の一行は「干渉部」であり、もう一行は「基底部」である。基底部は俳句的基本内容で、干渉部はその内容に場や指向を提供する部分である。

洪氏のこの俳句は十文字わずかであるが、詩歌芸術における最高の法則――「詩歌言語の構築」と一致すると思う。最近また五七五の漢文俳句を主張する派別が出てきているが、その内容は中国の古典詩から離れず、陳腐で新味のないものばかりである。この俳句の基本内容は秋の風。秋風は気体の流れで、形はないが感じとれる。その中で詩人は「物のひとつ」という驚異的な見方をする。つまり、詩人がその場で接触することのできる物のひとつということだ。秋風は物でもなければ、数えることもできない。この俳句が言いたいのは、全ての物など関係ない、秋風だけに魅了された、ということである。なんという力なき悲しみなのか。

秋風のどこに魅了されたのか。詩人はわずかな文字、「当てになる」でその意を明かした。「当てになる」の措辞は絶妙で、まったく悟りの深き詩人の用語

に属する。詩人は一人で秋風の中に立ち、掴みどころのない存在の茫然さに気づいた。今夜の灯、明日の城門、我はいづこやら。当てにならない人生は悲痛である。詩人は敢えて自分の当てになるものを明らかにしない。ぼくは二〇一六年にノーベル文学賞を受賞したボブディランの歌詞を思い出す…

The answer is blowing in the wind
答えは風に吹かれているよ

はっきりと言わない。それは詩における重要な技法である。それを支える理論はつまり、世間の物事を全て語ることはできない、全ての詩は世の一部分を呈示するのみだということに尽きる。秋風を当てになる物のひとつとするということは、詩人がまだ当てになる物はあるということを信じているということになる。秋風の他にも、その二、その三はある。しかし、今の時点で、彼女はまだそれらを発見していない。この俳句は悲しいながらも、希望に満ち溢れている。この俳句の全ての文字が宝石のように輝き、新味ともつれ合う意向で、余韻を無限に醸

142

し出している。俳句は目ではなく、心で読むという真髄を語る一句である。

二〇一九年八月二十二日

世界華文作家交流協会詩学顧問

秀実

秀実氏プロフィール

世界華文作家交流協会詩学顧問，香港詩歌協会会長，「圓桌詩刊」編集長。「香港中文文学詩歌賞」、「新北市文学賞新詩賞」、「昌耀詩歌賞」など、数多くの賞を受賞。詩集に「紙屑」、「昭陽殿記事」、「臺北翅膀」、「像貓一様孤寂 *Lonely as My Moggy*」；散文集に「九個城塔」、「小鎮一夜蟲喧」、「某個休士頓女子」；評論集に「劉半農詩歌研究」、「散文詩的蛹與蝶」、「我捉住飛翔的尾巴」、「為詩一辯」などがある。編集の著作に「燈火隔河守望——深港詩選」、「無邊夜色——寧港詩選」、「大海在其南——潮港詩選」、「風過松濤與麥浪——台港愛情詩精粋」などがある。

143

附錄三 華文俳句的寫作方法

華文俳句（以下簡稱「俳句」）的寫作方法說明如下：

一、俳句無題，分兩行。

　　例：

　　　　古池啊！

　　　　青蛙跳入水聲響

　　　　　　　　　　　　　　　　　　　　※松尾芭蕉（1644-1694）

144

二、第一行和第二行之間意思斷開，即日本俳句的「切」。二行間的關係，我們稱之為「二項組合」。二者不即不離，一重一輕，一主一次，由相互的關聯、襯托、張力來營造詩意。

　　例：

　　　　地球彷彿那方

　　　　魚鱗雲

　　　　　　　　　　　　　　　　　　　　　　　　　　※洪郁芬

三、我們提倡一首俳句用一個季語，即表示季節的詞語。

　　例：

　　　　秋日高空

　　　　驚嘆號的台北一〇一大樓

　　　　　　　　　　　　　　　　　　　　　　　　　　※郭至卿

四、俳句內容須吟詠當下、截取瞬間。不寫過去和將來。

例：

釣竿動也不動

蜻蜓點水

※趙紹球

五、吟詠具體的事物。不寫抽象。

例：

早春還寒

浮世畫的逆捲波

※永田滿德

146

六、提倡簡約、留白。儘量不用多餘或說明性的詞語。

青嶺

例：

龍王出入的雲霄

※五島高資

二〇一九年七月吉日

洪郁芬、郭至卿、趙紹球、吳衛峰

付録三　華文俳句の書き方

以下、華文俳句を俳句と称して説明する。

（一）俳句にタイトルはない。二行に書く。

　　例：

　　古池や

　　蛙飛び込む水の音

　　　　　　　　　　※松尾芭蕉（1644-1694）

（二）一行目と二行目の間に切れがある。二行の関係は取り合わせで、つかず離れず、共に詩意を醸し出す。

例：

うろこ雲

向こうに地球あるやうな

※洪郁芬

（三）一句の俳句に季語一つを提唱する。

例：

驚嘆符の台北一〇一ビル

秋の空

※郭至卿

（四）今を読む。瞬間を切り取る。

　　例：
　　水面をかすめる蜻蛉
　　動かぬ釣り竿

※趙紹球

（五）具体的な物を詠む。

　　例：
　　浮世絵の波の逆巻き
　　寒戻る

※永田満徳

（六）用語は少なく。

例：

わたつみの雲居に通う

青嶺かな

※五島高資

二〇一九年七月吉日

洪郁芬、郭至卿、趙紹球、吳衛峰

ちっぽけな光の調べ草の露　郁芬

日本書法家　梨華

CONTENTS

Preface 1

Same as the international department of Japan Haiku University who advocates "Cut" and "Toriawase ", the Taiwanese publication of *Tune of Tiny Light*, Yuhfen Hong's personal Chinese haiku anthology, is worth celebrating.

Haiku is one of the traditional Japanese poetry. Now crossing the Japanese fence, haiku is written in different languages around the world, and has become an international literary style. However, looking at the reality of international haiku, we observe that most of the international haikus are written in three lines without the manifestation of the essence of haiku aesthetics. This is because the international haiku did not reach a consensus on the form and characteristics of haiku.

In order to promote "Cut" and "Toriawase (Juxtaposition)", which are the essence of haiku in the Chinese circle, I worked as a consultant and co-author of *Chinese Haiku Selection* in the publication of Yuhfen Hong, Kuo Chih Ching, Steven Chew and

Wu Weifeng in December 2018. In addition, I also served as a consultant to the "Chinese Haiku Society" , which was established on December 4, 2018, to promote the development of Chinese Haiku.

As a consultant to the "Chinese Haiku Society", I am quite happy to see the President of Chinese Haiku Society, Yuhfen Hong published *Tune of Tiny Light*. I hope that the publication of this Chinese haiku anthology will enable readers to better understand the haiku aesthetics of "Cut" and "Toriawase." I hope that Chinese Haiku can work with classical poetry, modern poetry, short poetry and prose poetry to enrich the circle of Chinese poetry.

> Let grasshoppers fly and march on
> a thousand miles grassland

This is the haiku of Yuhfen Hong selected in the the second Nihyaku-toka Haiku Contest in Japan. Being able to receive a prize among professional Japanese haijins not only proves that her Japanese literacy is profound, but also illustrates her extraordinary haiku art. In recent years, Yuhfen's haikus have been published in *Kasin* haiku quarterly in Japan. At the 65th *Kasin* haiku quarterly,

her haiku, "tune of tiny light / grass dew" was commented by *Kasin*'s Chief Editor, Junko Imamura. Imamura commented that "Yuhfen described the corn-like light of grass dew as 'tiny', and find out the rhythm contained in dew's light. We are aware of her unique observation and delicate emotions."

> chirps of birds
> set off the awakened ferry

> When I twist the lid of glass bottles
> near summer

> autumn sunny day
> open the door with a sign

These above haikus, no matter in the content or in the Toriawase of the seasonal word, are no less than the Japanese formal haiku. I dare to assert that Yuhfen Hong is fully in line with the conditions that can be developed in the Japanese haiku community.

end of love

fallen black wings of termites

first reading of the New Testament

words of love

These haikus make us feel the vivid youthful vitality of Yuhfen Hong, which is a feature of her haiku. In addition to the "end" of love, also in the haiku "a floc of dandelion / end of grassland in the dream", there are many "ends" in her haikus, for examples:

at the end of the mountain road end

cherry blossom bloomed

blue sea at the end of the mountain road

first trip of the year

For her "end" preferences and pursuits, it can be said that the same is true for her preferences for "the other side" or "the other shore". There is even a strong interest and inclination towards the "end of the world."

mackerel clouds

the earth is beyond

entangling afterlife and this life

winter mist

From these two haikus, we seem to enter Yuhfen Hong's spiritual garden, paved with haikus. The religious beliefs in the lines or the perception of the afterlife can also be said to be a feature of her haiku.

Finally, I list here the haikus that I admire:

garden there and I

continuous fall of petals

catch my childhood

swing at the highest point

to be light at full strength

butterflies fly

Children fought and broke dishes

heat wave

July, 2019

Mitsunori NAGATA

Vice President of Japan Haiku Association

Presentation of Mitsunori NAGATA

Born in Japan, 1954. Vice President of Japan Haiku Association, President of Haiku University, editor of *Kasin* haiku quarterly, administrative secretary of Japan Haijin Association. Collections of haiku: *Kanmaturi*. Co-author of *100 Souseki Kumamoto* and *New Kumamoto Saijiki*.

Preface II

The name, Tune of Tiny Light, originates from one of my haikus in the Japanese *Kasin* haiku quarterly, "tune of tiny light / grass dew". Let's not talk about the literal meaning in my work. Instead, let's talk about the start of Chinese haiku. Compared to the majority of traditional and new Chinese poetic writing, the small number of haiku writing is like a speck of dust. Haiku is a cultural heritage imparted to Taiwan during the Japanese colonial period, when it was a social pastime for the older elite and a choice for modern poets who wanted to write shorter poems. Within the huge expanse of traditional Chinese literature, Chinese haiku is a super minority. However, what truly makes this colonial foreign literature so well known, unforgotten by time?

It seems unreasonable that we try to use colonial influence to explain how the development of haiku has become a global trend. Since the latter half of 19th century, Japanese scholars who studied in the West have established an international reputation of an

unbelievable scale for haiku. Over the centuries, haiku has survived the changes of time, and has further thrived in the literature of many countries to this day, keeping many foreigners busy with delving into the possibilities of haiku with their local languages. Recently, a Swedish haiku poet, Tomas Tranströmer, became the winner of the Nobel Prize in Literature, which has helped the global upward trend of haiku. Therefore, the influence of haiku has expanded and become an internationally common form of literature.

Back to *Tune of Tiny Light*. Dew on grass is tiny, just like the shortness of Chinese haiku. Among "one of the shortest haiku in the world", Chinese haiku is short and small, like sand on the beach. The form of Chinese haiku proposed by Zhan Bing is written in the 3-4-3 form with 10 characters. Chinese haikus are normally written in 2 lines, with no strict limits to length—short and long lines are acceptable. Let's look at the beginning of summer in the book for example. One of the haikus is "love or not / flowers turned into green leaves", which has a total of 7 Chinese characters. The other haiku related to the name of the book is "tune of tiny light / grass dew", which has a total of 6 Chinese characters. Of course, we cannot judge a Chinese haiku with word counts like we would other forms of poetry. Poems are the emotional stirrings of the heart, and

the streaming light that flows through the words.

Tone of light in an autumn morning, as I walk around a private farm, surrounded by a dense fog, I looked into a road mirror and saw only a reflection of fog. The surrounding mountains were half hidden by the fog and intermittently showed themselves until they completely faded into gray. Wandering in the gray silent world with my own shadow, I saw the grass covered by the heavy grain-like dew glistening in the tone of light. The melody was mellifluous, just like a twinkling star was the greatest praise to the All Mighty. At that moment, I thought about haiku. In our busy lives, our minds are often bothered by busy thoughts. As a result, we are not able to notice the wind, flower, grass, and the moon that come with seasonal changes, paying attention solely to daily quarrels. Sometimes, we excessively focus on enumerating what we lost in the past, rather than enjoying the moment and embracing the beautiful scenery. However, if we are willing to slow down our pace, take a look at every tiny details in our lives, and try to look on the brighter side, we will be able to write a beautiful haiku with all the things we observe from the seasons. All these moving moments are just like the tone of light shining on that dew, which brings a distinctive melody to life and becomes proof of

our existence.

As Henri-Louis Bergson said, life is decided by the time of memory or perception. When we lose ourselves in the experience of the instant, the fleeting instant is immediately given an eternal meaning. Thus, we are able to free ourselves from the restrictions of time and express the enthusiasm of life in every instant. Haiku is a form of literature that can capture inspiration at every moment and make it eternal. The poets of haiku observe everything in life and try to grasp the true nature of the beauty within. This is a part of Japanese aesthetics called *mono no aware*. Falling petals and leaves, swaying pine and crops. In a short and fragile life, only the observation of the fleeting instant is proof of existence. *Kigo* (seasonal words), which change on the basis of a year, let us be truly aware of the flow of time. *Kire* (Cut) let us slow down our pace and start to observe and hear the pulsations of nature. The haiku we write will also draw the sympathy of those who pay attention to language and art, just like how the tone of light affected me.

Masaoka Shiki, Japanese haiku poet, once stood for the conception of *Shasei* (sketching). Masaoka said that throughout the history of Japanese literature, subjective aesthetics dominated

the ancient times; on the contrary, we, nowadays, focus more on the expression of objective aesthetics. "Indirect description is a feeling for the results; an objective matter that is solely focused on description as reason moves the heart of the reader." When we are concentrating on the outside, the true nature of the inner and outer worlds harmonize as one. Our existence vanishes and the consciousness attains a tremendous brightness, and eventually, we mingle with the universe. We are part of nature, and so nature exists in us. Thus, the tree is you and you are the tree. We break the barriers between consciousness and body, which brings the eternal and harmony tone of light. That's the great spirit given by haiku, even though it is just as puny as dew on grass.

I am looking forward to the publication of this book, and I hope that this book can help you understand more about Chinese haiku, help slow your pace, and turn all of your instants into eternity. Finally, please allow me to end the preface with the famous quote from the beginning of William Blake's *Auguries of Innocence*:

> To see a World in a Grain of Sand
> And a Heaven in a Wild Flower

Hold Infinity in the palm of your hand

And Eternity in an hour

May, 2019

Yuhfen Hong

Epilogue I -
Commentary on Yuhfen Hong's Haiku
by Takatoshi GOTO

a dragon climbing into the sky

main lantern of the Love River

Love river is one of the largest rivers run across entire Kaohsiung city of southern Taiwan. Murmuring of running water corresponds to the dragon. I recalled a poem by Li-Bai, "Seeing off Meng Haoran Bound for Guangling / Till the Yangtze gushing towards the horizon was all that could be seen". As dragon's eye, the lights of lantern brighten up the skyline. The same season with Li-Bai's poem, Spring. The dragon is not only a river, but also a representative of all life. Author's heart climbs with lantern's light as the dragon goes into the sky. This Haiku is a fusion between human mind and the nature.

halfway to learn the celestial sound

voice of cicadas

Only a poet can hear the sounds by mind, and translate chirping of cicadas into voice. Corresponds to the bugs' songs, the mysteries of the nature. This Haiku contains sounds of people, earth, and celestial, which makes the reader deeply moved.

tune of tiny light

grass dew

The miracle of creation always starts from a tiny thing, such as grass. I'm enchanted by the author who can hear the tune from grass dew. Authors' haikus use a lot of connections between visual and sounds, which represents the true spirit of haiku, which we could also observe in Bashou Matsuo's haikus. In addition, this haiku contains "tune" which also corresponds to "lonesome" and "elegant", which are the essence of autumn. It is preciously due to short life time, which brings people touching. It is even hard for Japanese to master the profound meaning of haiku. I'm surprised with author's skill to haiku at this level, and sincerely looking

forward to seeing the development of her haiku in the future.

Presentation of Takatoshi GOTO

Born in Nagasaki city, Japan, May 23, 1968. Graduated from Jichi Medical University. Vice President of Japan Haiku Association, President of Haiku Square, editor of Monthly *Haiku World*, Vice President of Haiku University, member of Japanese Artists Association. Won the Nakashinden Sweden Haiku Prize in 1997, the Award for Modern Haiku Criticism in 2000 and so on. Collections of haiku: *Hippocampus*, *Thunderbolt* and so on.

Epilogue II -
Commentary on Yuhfen Hong's Haiku
by Xiu Shi – Autumn Wind Count

Yuhfen Hong published a haiku in the "Chinese Haiku Society" on August 20th:

> One of the things I can count on
>
> autumn wind

As one of the literary categories of Chinese poetry, Chinese Haiku is characterized by: two lines, the relationship between the two is Kire (Cut) and Kigo (seasonal word). I want to point out that Chinese haiku can be classified as Chinese modern poems regulated by certain rules. The situation is like Sonnet. There are both formal and content requirements. Sonnet is also known as the English poem consisting of one single fourteen-line stanza. The last two lines are often the essence of the whole poem, and they are inspiring

aphorisms. The first line of the Chinese haiku is "Interference part", and the last line is "Bottom part. " The latter is the basic content of the haiku, while the former is the background or direction provided to the basic content.

This Yuhfen Hong's haiku contains only ten words, but is in line with the highest law of poetry art: the construction of poetry language. At present, some people advocate the 5-7-5 style of the haiku written in Chinese, but their wordings are obsolete, and there is no new ideas. The basic content of this haiku is the autumn wind. The autumn wind is the flow of air, invisible and sensible. The poet mentioned an extremely amazing point, "one of the things", that is, one of the many things that the poet was in contact with. As we know, autumn wind can't be counted by quantity. Therefore, the underlying language of this haiku is that all things are irrelevant at the moment, except the charming autumn wind. So helpless and full of grief!

How charming is autumn wind? The poet provides clues in very limited text, "count on." These two words are extremely clever, and are terms of a savvy poet. She stood independently in autumn wind and felt the sorrow of existence. Tonight's lights and tomorrow's city gate. Where will I go? Life without hope is

sorrowful. Yet, she doesn't mention what she is counting on. I am reminded of the song of Bob Dylan, winner of the Nobel Prize in Literature in 2016, "The answer is blowing in the wind."

Implicitness is one of the most important techniques of poetry. The theory is that things in the world cannot be said, and all poems only partially present the world. Since autumn wind is one of the things that can be expected, there must be something else that can be expected as well. Just now she hasn't found it yet. Sorrow and hope are hidden in this haiku at the same time. Each word is a gem in this haiku, with renovating ideas, concealed entanglements and endless aftertaste. This is a good example of reading haiku with "heart" and not with "eyes."

August, 2019

Xiu Shi

Poetic Consultant to the World Chinese Writers

Association of Exchange Inc.

Presentation of Xiu Shi

Poetry consultant to the World Chinese Writers Association of Exchange Inc., President of the Hong Kong Poetry Club, and

founder and Editor-in-Chief of *The Roundtable*: A Journal of Poetry and Poetics, is a prolific writer and poet who has published in Hong Kong, Taiwan, and China. Recipient of the Hong Kong Chinese Literature Poetry Award (1986), the Chang Yao Poetry Award (2016), and the New Taipei City Literature Poetry Award (2016), he is the author of half a dozen volumes of poetry including *Scrap Paper*, *The Zhao-Yang Palace Chronicle*, *Wings of Taipei* and *Lonely as My Moggy*, as well as several collections of essays including *Nine City Towers*, *A Special Woman from Huston*, *A Defense of Poetry*, and *Butterflies Don't Dream*. He is also the editor of *Selected Poetry from Shenzhen* and *Hong Kong and Essential Loves Poems from Hong Kong and Taiwan*.

Epilogue III - Writing Methods of Chinese Haiku

1. Chinese Haiku is untitled and is divided into two lines.

    e.g.

    old pond

    sound of a frog leaping into the water

    ※Matsuo Bashō (1644-1694)

2. The disconnection of meaning between the first line and the second line is the "Cut" of the Japanese haiku. The relationship between the two lines is what we call the "Toriawase." The poetry is created by mutual association, setting and tension.

e.g.

mackerel clouds

the earth is beyond

※ Yuhfen Hong

3. We advocate one Kigo (seasonal word) in a haiku.

e.g.

Taipei 101 building is an exclamation mark

autumn sky

※ Kuo Chih Ching

4. The content of a haiku must describe a moment at present. Do not write the past and the future.

e.g.

a dragonfly skimming the surface of the water

still fishing rod

※ Steven Chew

5. Write concrete things. Do not write abstractions.

    e.g.

    the reverse waves of Ukiyoe

    early spring turned cold again

※Mitsunori NAGATA

6. Promote simplicity and leave blank. Try not to use redundant or descriptive words.

    e.g.

    blue mountains

    Watatsumi comes and goes into the cloudy sky

※Takatoshi GOTO

July, 2019

Yuhfen Hong

Kuo Chih Ching

Steven Chew

Wu Weifeng

華文俳句叢書1　PG2330

 渺光之律
　　　——華文俳句集

作　　　者	洪郁芬
責任編輯	洪聖翔
圖文排版	周妤靜
封面設計	趙紹球

出版策劃	釀出版
製作發行	秀威資訊科技股份有限公司
	114 台北市內湖區瑞光路76巷65號1樓
	電話：+886-2-2796-3638　傳真：+886-2-2796-1377
	服務信箱：service@showwe.com.tw
	http://www.showwe.com.tw
郵政劃撥	19563868　戶名：秀威資訊科技股份有限公司
展售門市	國家書店【松江門市】
	104 台北市中山區松江路209號1樓
	電話：+886-2-2518-0207　傳真：+886-2-2518-0778
網路訂購	秀威網路書店：https://store.showwe.tw
	國家網路書店：https://www.govbooks.com.tw
法律顧問	毛國樑　律師
總 經 銷	聯合發行股份有限公司
	231新北市新店區寶橋路235巷6弄6號4F
	電話：+886-2-2917-8022　傳真：+886-2-2915-6275

出版日期	2019年10月　BOD一版
定　　　價	220元

Printed in Taiwan

國家圖書館出版品預行編目

渺光之律：華文俳句集 / 洪郁芬作. -- 一版. --
臺北市：釀出版, 2019.10
　　面；　公分. -- (華文俳句叢書；1)
　　BOD版
　　中日英對照
　　ISBN 978-986-445-350-4(平裝)

863.51　　　　　　　　　　108013954

讀 者 回 函 卡

感謝您購買本書，為提升服務品質，請填妥以下資料，將讀者回函卡直接寄回或傳真本公司，收到您的寶貴意見後，我們會收藏記錄及檢討，謝謝！
如您需要了解本公司最新出版書目、購書優惠或企劃活動，歡迎您上網查詢或下載相關資料：http:// www.showwe.com.tw

您購買的書名：＿＿＿＿＿＿＿＿＿＿＿＿＿＿＿＿＿＿＿＿＿＿＿

出生日期：＿＿＿＿＿＿年＿＿＿＿＿＿月＿＿＿＿＿＿日

學歷：□高中 (含) 以下　　□大專　　□研究所 (含) 以上

職業：□製造業　□金融業　□資訊業　□軍警　□傳播業　□自由業
　　　□服務業　□公務員　□教職　　□學生　□家管　□其它＿＿＿

購書地點：□網路書店　□實體書店　□書展　□郵購　□贈閱　□其他

您從何得知本書的消息？

　　□網路書店　□實體書店　□網路搜尋　□電子報　□書訊　□雜誌
　　□傳播媒體　□親友推薦　□網站推薦　□部落格　□其他＿＿＿＿＿

您對本書的評價：(請填代號　1.非常滿意　2.滿意　3.尚可　4.再改進)

　　封面設計＿＿＿　版面編排＿＿＿　內容＿＿＿　文／譯筆＿＿＿　價格＿＿＿

讀完書後您覺得：

　　□很有收穫　□有收穫　□收穫不多　□沒收穫

對我們的建議：＿＿＿＿＿＿＿＿＿＿＿＿＿＿＿＿＿＿＿＿＿＿＿
＿＿＿＿＿＿＿＿＿＿＿＿＿＿＿＿＿＿＿＿＿＿＿＿＿＿＿＿＿＿＿
＿＿＿＿＿＿＿＿＿＿＿＿＿＿＿＿＿＿＿＿＿＿＿＿＿＿＿＿＿＿＿
＿＿＿＿＿＿＿＿＿＿＿＿＿＿＿＿＿＿＿＿＿＿＿＿＿＿＿＿＿＿＿

11466
台北市內湖區瑞光路 76 巷 65 號 1 樓

秀威資訊科技股份有限公司　　　收

BOD 數位出版事業部

（請沿線對折寄回，謝謝！）

姓　　名：＿＿＿＿＿＿＿＿　年齡：＿＿＿＿　性別：□女　□男

郵遞區號：□□□□□

地　　址：＿＿＿＿＿＿＿＿＿＿＿＿＿＿＿＿＿＿＿＿＿＿

聯絡電話：(日)＿＿＿＿＿＿＿＿＿　(夜)＿＿＿＿＿＿＿＿＿＿

E - m a i l：＿＿＿＿＿＿＿＿＿＿＿＿＿＿＿＿＿＿＿＿＿